It Only Takes One Friend...

by Robin Taylor-Chiarello

Illustrated by Lisa Bohart

Edited by Jane Brandi Johnson

Library of Congress Control Number: 2013906219

Printed in the U.S.A.
Printed by Knockout www.knockoutpub.com

Printed May 2013

BEECH HILL FARM
& BISON RANCH

For Benjamin Traynor:

You moved to a new town, enrolled in a new school, made many friends, and became an important part of the baseball team! You accepted the challenge. Most important, you are a perfect example that.....
It Only Takes One Friend to make you feel at home!

With admiration and friendship,
Robin

"I leave the ranch in Greenville, Maine knowing my life will not be the same."

4

"It's an honor, they say, that I am going to meet the head bison at Beech Hill– his name is Big Chief."

"He's old and tired— just wants to move on.
So, I'm his replacement beginning at dawn."

The journey began at sunrise today,
boarding the truck to be driven away.

I said goodbye to the friends I hold dear.
"Hope to see you in a couple of years!"

With a bump, bump, bump on Route 135,
a bump, bump, bump– "Oh, what a ride!"

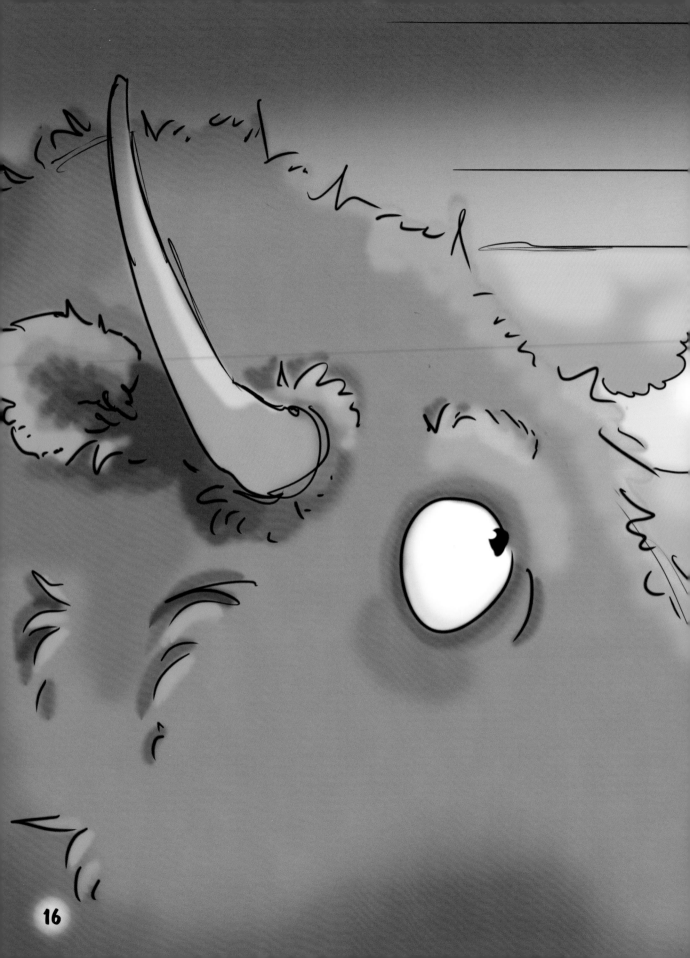

I looked out the window on the side of the truck.
"Where are we going? We've just passed a duck!"

BEECH HILL FARM
& BISON RANCH

A bump, bump, bump, and a sign, Bolsters Mill.
"This can't be right...my new home's on a hill."

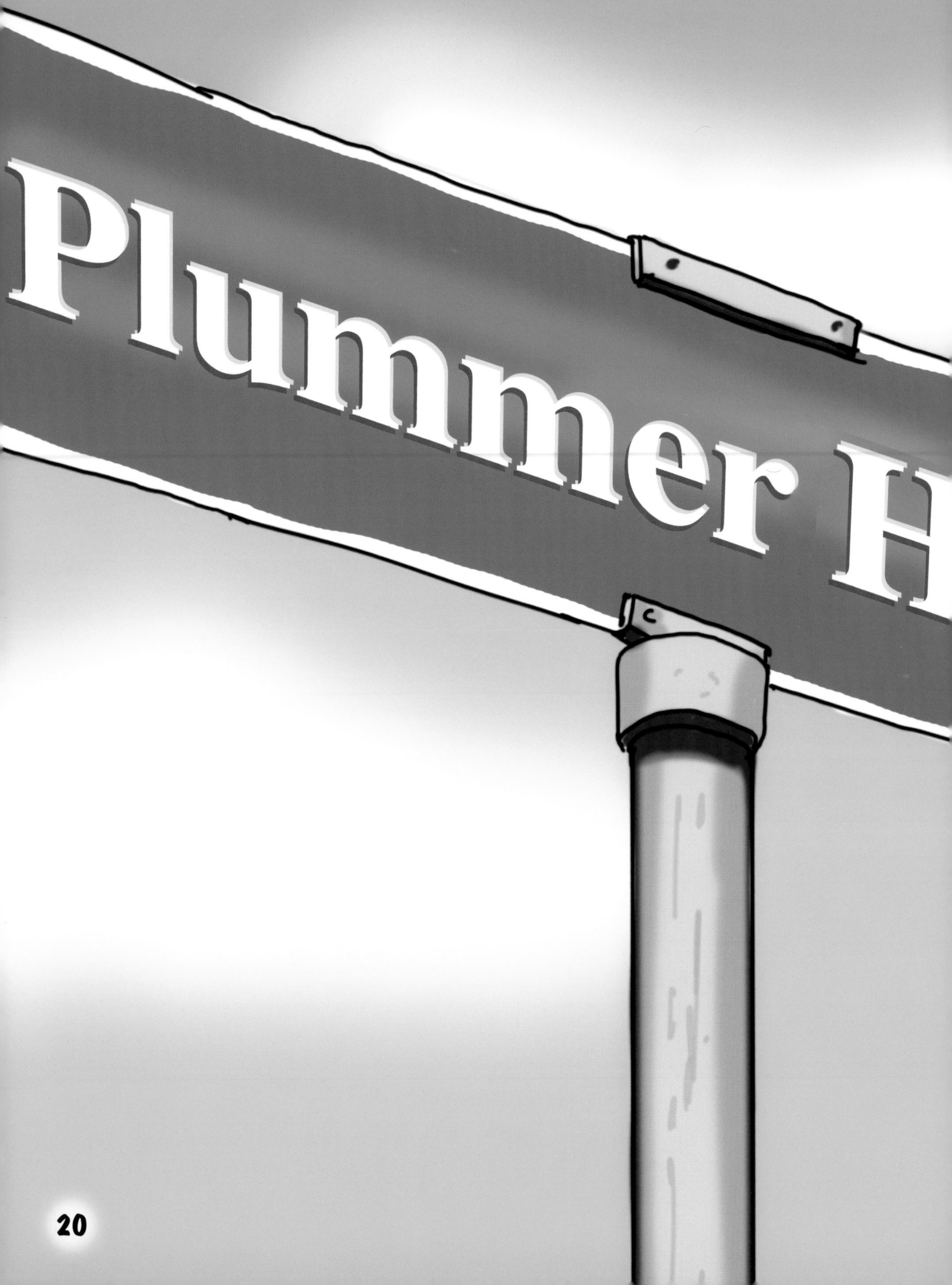
Plummer H

Then just before Plummer Hill Road,
the driver yells out, "It's time to unload!"

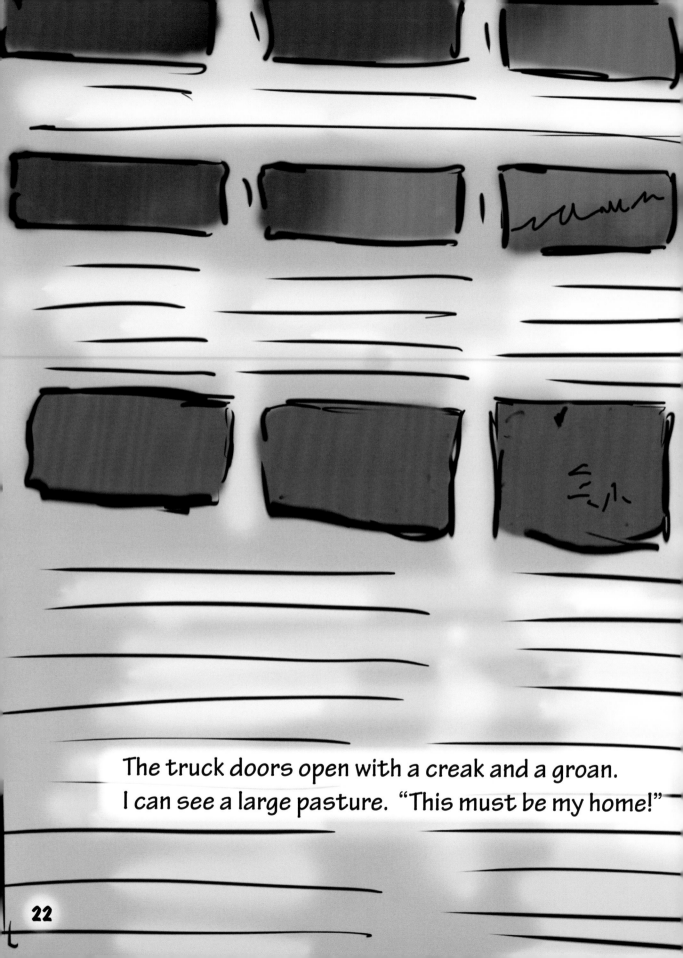

The truck doors open with a creak and a groan. I can see a large pasture. "This must be my home!"

Rich green grass and two mineral licks,
"I could learn to like this, pretty darn quick!"

"Hello Little Chief, I'm Abigail Frizzle.
Excuse my appearance, but it's starting to drizzle."

"I arrived at Beech Hill just eight months ago after being purchased at a fall poultry show."

28

29

"I was supposed to be an award-winning hen,
but my feathers grew outward and curled up to my chin!"

"Beech Hill is fun; folks are nice on this hill.
Visitors come often which gives us a thrill."

BEECH HILL FARM
& BISON RANCH

"Moving to a new place shouldn't be hard.
I'll take you around… we'll tour the barnyard."

"I'll tell you about the life on this farm.
It's a crazy place with all kinds of charm."

"The owners– Ted, Doretta, and Sandy the cat–
live in the big house with an occasional bat."

"Chicks on the hill in the Chick Chick Chalet,
cackle and scratch just passing the day."

40

'cock a doodle

io'

"Do-Little the Rooster crows, Cock a doodle doo!
and the fawn-and-white Guernsey adds, Cock a doodle moo!

"Kestrel flies fast overhead to his nest,
yelling a klee as the sun's setting west."

"Peep the Barred Owl, keeps watch with one eye.
You might faintly see him in a well-moonlit sky."

46

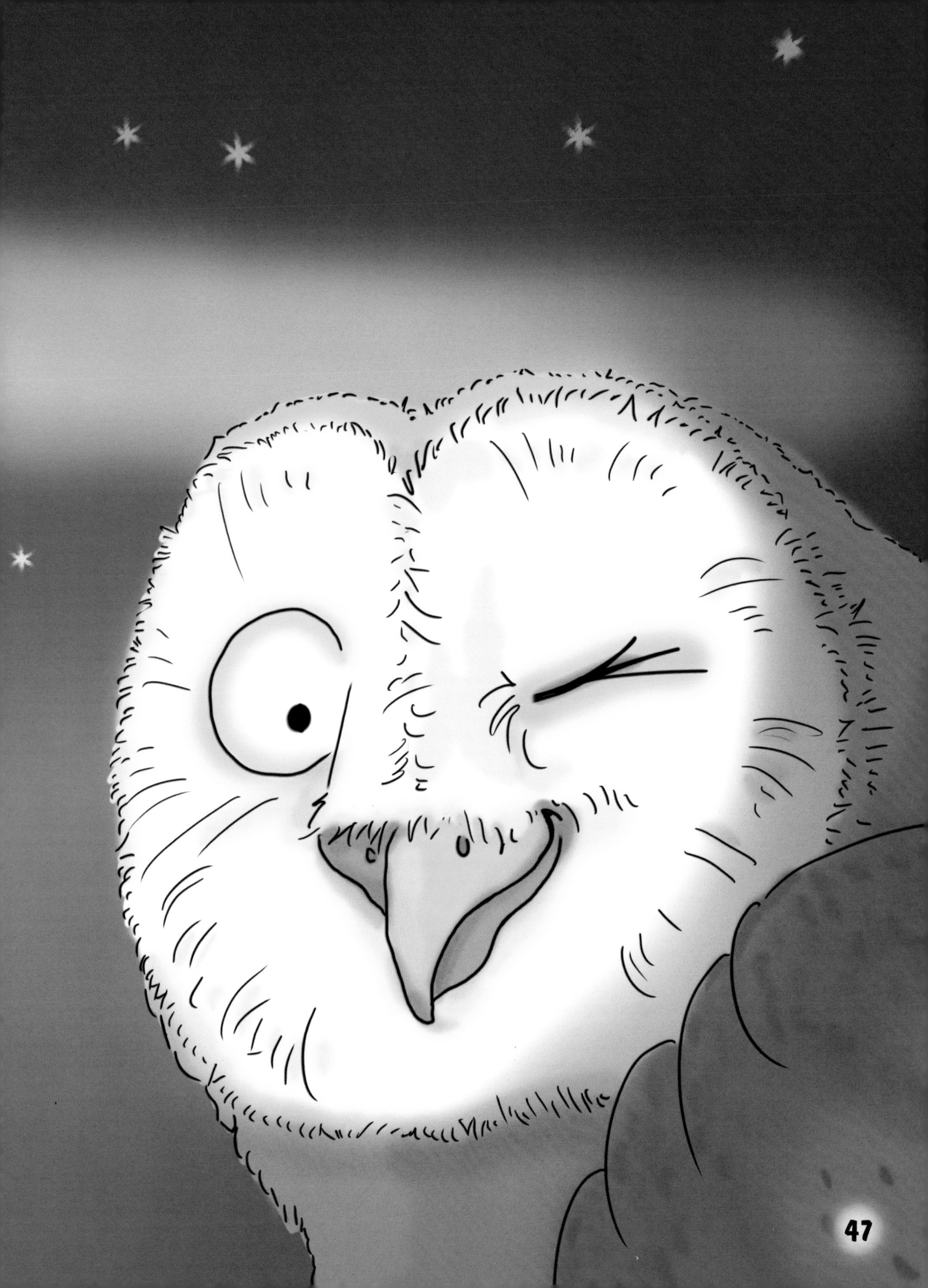

as you stand in the field and look toward the trees,
 he sweet smell of baked breads will drift through the breeze!"

"Marta the chef, is baking today…
her three-berry pie is Maine's best, people say!"

50

"She may walk toward the fence, leave an apple to eat,
or bring you a baked good as a real special treat."

"You'll live in the pasture to the west of the barn.
The four lady bisons will be thrilled by your charm."

"There is Summer, Laura, Ginger, and Belle.
They can't wait to meet you and wish you well."

"You'll make friends quite fast— I know that you wi
Everyone's been waiting to meet our herd bull."

"Well thank you Miss Frizzle, the pleasure is mine.
I'll be living at this ranch for a very long time."

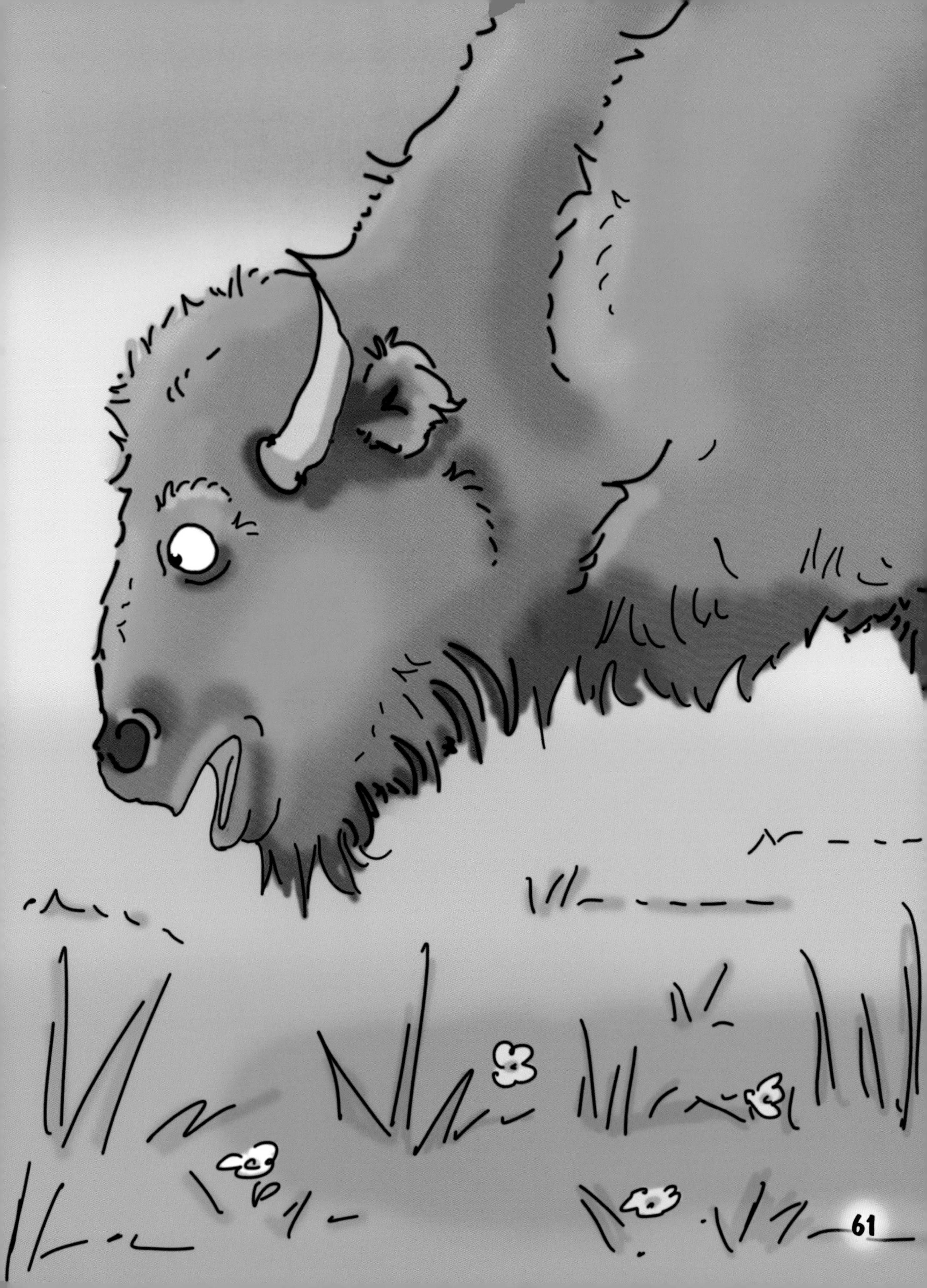

"I can run 35, throw hay in the air;
it's a great bison sport... I have not a care."

"Jump toward the sun, it's all really neat–
an amazing accomplishment for a guy with big feet."

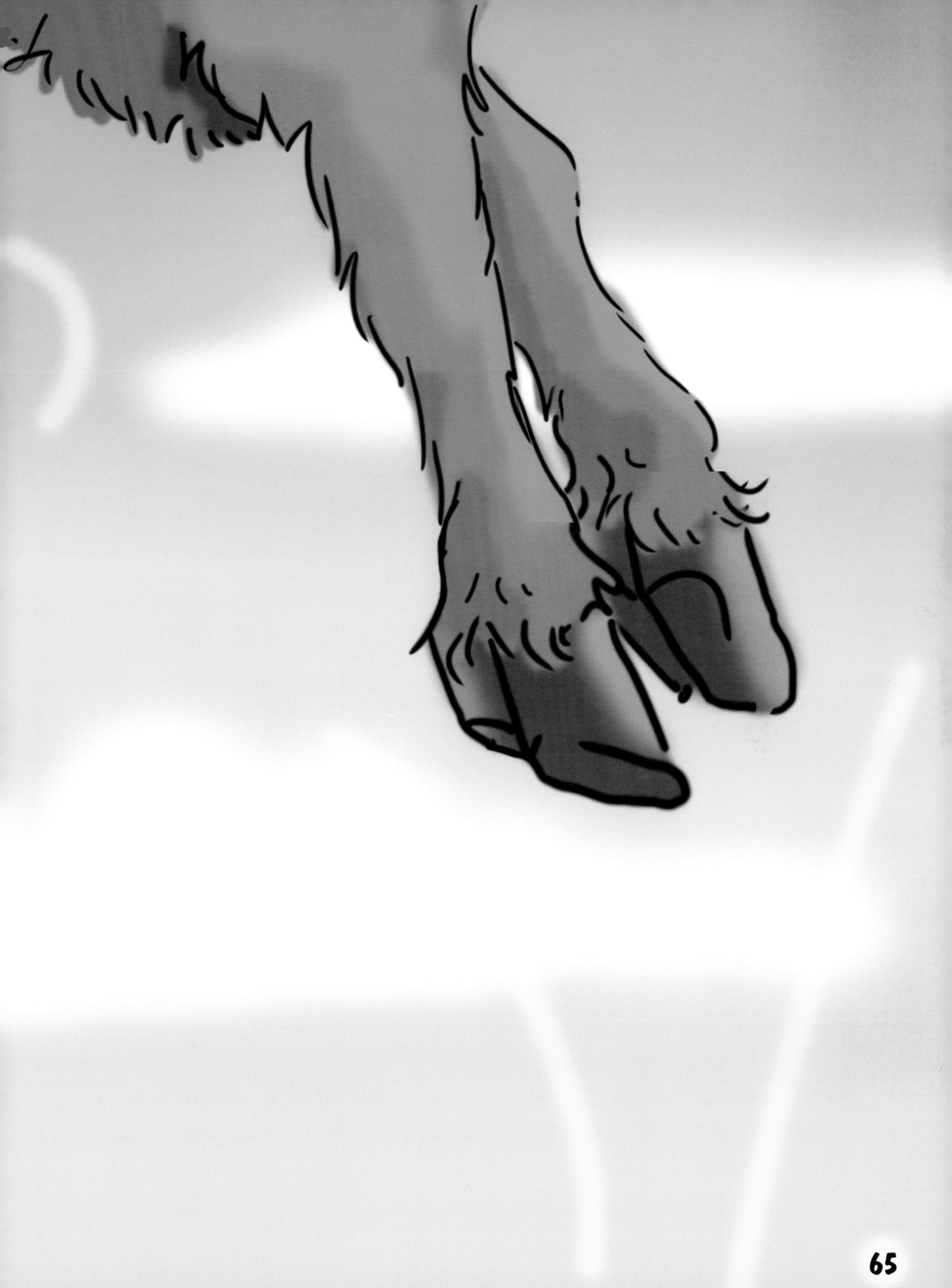

"Thank you Abigail, you are a true friend.
You've made me feel very happy again."

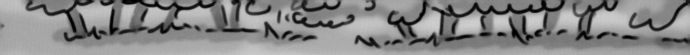

"Making one friend when you move can be hard, but I feel like I know this entire barnyard."

"I was feeling so sad to be new and alone,
but your very warm welcome makes me feel

The End.

Dear Little Chief,

Bentley, a puppy who is arriving today,
has left Vermont and is on his way. He will
not know anyone here who can play...so, please
remember what it's like to be new, and do for
him what I did for you.

Your friend from the barnyard,

Abigail Avis Frizzle

New words from Little Chief

Appearance: The way something looks

Barnyard: Area of open ground around a barn

Barred Owl: Large owl native to North America

Cackle: A clucking cry

Chalet: Type of shelter

Drizzle: Light rain

Frizzle: Type of chicken whose feathers curl outward

Guernsey: Cow that produces milk

Herd Bull: Male bull used for reproducing the breed

Kestrel: A bird of prey; member of the falcon family

Klee: The sound a Kestrel makes

Mineral Lick: A natural mineral deposit where animals can obtain nutrients

Pasture: Land covered with grass for cattle and sheep

Replacement: A substitute

" A wonderful message for
children who face the challenge
of moving to a new town
or school."

" There's a lot to learn from a
chicken with feathers gone wild!"

" A heartwarming story about
the importance of friendship."

" Another great message from
Award-winning author,
Robin Taylor-Chiarello."

" Much more than a story about
animals on a farm! It's about the
positive impact of having a good
friend!"

" A warm and loving story with
a poignant message."

My thanks to Ted and Doretta Colburn,
owners of Beech Hill Farm and Bison Ranch.
The farm is a special place where man and
beast live in harmony in the shadows of
the White Mountains.
-- Robin Taylor Chiarello--